The Red Knife Plays

by Adam Van Winkle

adapted from the Appalachian Gothic of
Sheldon Lee Compton

Cowboy Jamboree Press
good grit lit.

First Edition

ISBN: 9798562625038

www.cowboyjamboreemagazine.com

Cover and Interior Design: Steve Townes

Cowboy Jamboree Press good grit lit.

for Preston Jones

"Dang."
-Sheldon Lee Compton

<u>**Herein**</u>

The Mason Jar

an almost tragedy in 3 acts

(adapted from the novel <u>Dysphoria</u>
by Sheldon Lee Compton)

Characters

<u>Paul Shannon</u>: early 30s, average to slight build
<u>Uncle Hill Shannon</u>: late 50s with the paunch of middle age, his clothes are threadbare and worn shades lighter than their original intent
<u>Grandma Eve Shannon</u>: late 70s, worn and tired, but generally cheerful, wears pink
<u>Grandpa William Shannon</u>: late 70s, worn and tired, but generally cheerful, wears blue
<u>David Shannon</u>: in flashback to his raising Paul, he bears striking resemblance to adult Paul, though usually in khaki and navy work clothes
<u>Young Paul</u>: in flashback, 8 or 9 years old, slight build
<u>Gypsy Cab Driver</u>: a rough 40-something; has constant dip of snuff in front bottom lip; the appearance of his clothes is enough to create a putrid body odor
<u>John Harper</u>: late 70s, brighter than Grandma and Grandpa Shannon, though the social mannerisms and directness of someone who lives reclusive; clothes of a higher tick, though just as aged as everyone else's
<u>Larry Fenner</u>: a hulking man, mid-50s, with nervous eyes and ticks; always fidgeting; the way he wears overalls suggests a man-child in a beast's body
<u>Younger Eve Shannon</u>: mid 50s with a similar demeanor to Eve in the present, wears pink, can be played by same actress as the older in a pinch
<u>Younger William Shannon</u>: mid 50s with a similar demeanor to William in the present,

wears blue, can be played by same actor as
the older in a pinch
<u>Young Dave</u>: 12, average to slightly lean
build
<u>Young Hill</u>: 13, average to slightly lean
build
<u>Young Larry</u>: 12, though much larger than his
young friends David, Hill, and Tommy
<u>Young Tommy</u>: 12, average to slightly lean
build
<u>Joe Fenner</u>: rough 40s, stained, disheveled
clothes, lean and mean
<u>Clara Fenner:</u> rough 40s, stained, disheveled
clothes, as big or bigger than her husband

A Note on Staging

In the background is a large mural, faded and gray, of misty Kentucky ridges, an abandoned tipple the only black and unnatural object in the ghostly landscape. It remains background to every scene, minimalist interiors dominated by the Kentucky hills and the tipple. Exterior shots can be empty stage in front of the mural, or include simple indicators, like a scaffold to represent the tipple, or a simple fence row to indicate looking to a field. Interiors are similar between the three house settings, so much so the Fenner household should just be the reverse of walls of the Shannon household. Practically, the stage needs to be fairly sparse so that characters in the present can "look to a memory" down stage right or left in spotlight without obstruction.

Interior Sets

The Shannon house: an open kitchen, with a hallway connecting to a bedroom and bathroom. The kitchen has a table and four chairs, and door outside. The bedroom needs only the bed and a shelf above the head with what-nots. The bathroom needs a tub and hamper. 3 wall construction
Uncle Hill's trailerhouse: singlewide; elevated from the stage as a trailer on cinder blocks; 3-wall construction; on the stage in the "yard" around the trailer are handmade, faded signs: "Hillman's Car and Truck Parts" and "Elect Shannon"

The shed: old wood-paneled, dirt floor shack;
3 wall construction; one shelf, with a Mason
Jar of green beans and a can of food or two
The Fenner house: the Shannon house walls
literally just flip to reveal slightly
different, more dilapidated interior house
The Gypsy Cab: a rusted out, pieced together
country taxi cab, mostly open though should
be of real car parts

Exterior Sets

a fence row
a mine tipple scaffold: the boys climb and
fall off the stage downstage right, a ladder
comes up the front of the stage to the
scaffold, a mattress there for the fall
a rough porch set
David Shannon gravesite

Basic Sets

The Mason Jar
Act 1 Staging
backstage
Kentucky ridges with abandoned tipple mural
porch with door into kitchen
Gypsy Taxi Cab
bathroom
bedroom
Shannon Household
kitchen
hallway
fencerow
partial tipple and scaffold
The Mason Jar
Act 2 Staging
backstage
Kentucky ridges with abandoned tipple mural
the Fenner shed
Uncle Hill's Trailerhouse
the Fenner porch
partial tipple and scaffold

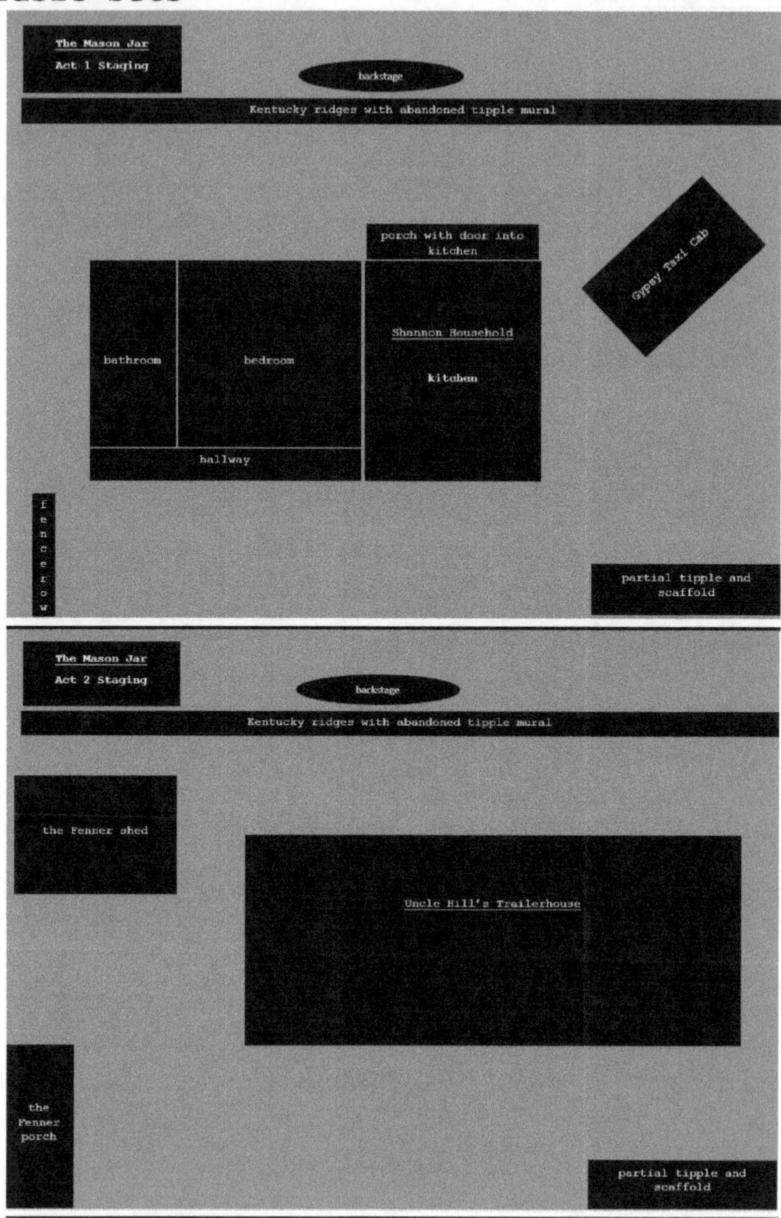

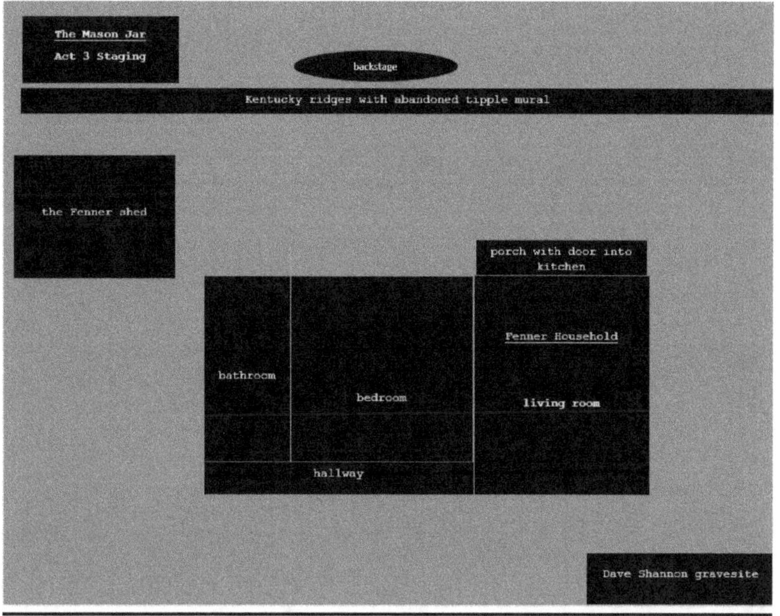

Note: The shed rotates from act 2 to act 3 so that the door of the shed is always toward the Fenner porch; the actors walk off the porch toward the shed in the same manner, it's just that this is in different position as the entire Fenner household is moved to center stage for act 3; the shed should also be designed so that it can be made more dilapidated (i.e. lean and/or have missing boards) for the latter scenes of act 3.

Act 1, Scene 1

In total darkness there is a 21-gun salute
sound effects; stark, abrasive, jarring for
the audience.

As the light comes up Paul Shannon sits at
his grandparents' kitchen table alone, with a
cup of coffee as his Uncle Hill comes in the
door without knocking, as this is his
parent's house, the house where he grew up.
Uncle Hill wears Goodwill funeral clothes, a
style he doesn't normally don, made apparent
by the white athletic socks he wears with his
wingtips and too short pants. Hill is
carrying a Ball Mason jar filled with loose
bills and a folded piece of legal pad paper.

HILL. (*Trying to be jovial on a sad
occasion.*) Don't I clean up pretty?

PAUL. (*Amused but with a clear pall of
obligatory sadness.*) Everything but that
face.

HILL. (*Laughs and pats Paul's shoulder as he
puts the jar and note in front of Paul which
neither really acknowledge.*) You should come
over before you head back. Your mom doing
okay?

PAUL. Yeah Mom's okay. You know her. She
takes it on the chin.

HILL. Hell yea she does. (*He takes his hand
off Paul, wanting to say something more, but
uncertain of what.*) I gotta go, find some
trouble. Good seeing you, Paul, even if…

PAUL. You, too, Uncle Hill, even if.

Hill exits the door. A shitty pickup
starting-up and pulling away is heard after a
few beats. Paul looks at the jar and note on
the table, gives a half smile at them, then
collects both as he stands and moves into the
bedroom while the light follows him. There
are magazines and books scattered, pill
bottles on the nightstand. His father's last
room, where he was found, the one he'd lived
in most of his life. Paul sets the jar on the
bed, and unfolds the letter as he sits next
to it on the bed. He begins to read aloud,
"I'm sorry…" as the light fades on Paul on
the bed in the bedroom and comes up again in
the kitchen next door where now Young Eve and
Young William sit with their grown son,
David, and his 8-year-old son, Paul.

Young Paul is trying to scrape every morsel
of his favorite dish, the mashed potatoes,
off his plate, knowing there are no extras.
As he does so, David is clearly annoyed with
his son and stares David down while David
continues on without notice. William and Eve
have the antsy nature of parents watching
their grown child raise his own child. Paul
is not trying to be annoying, but doesn't
realize the message his scraping fork
conveys. David grows to a near boil
watching.

Suddenly David erupts, throwing his chair
back as he stands and lunges for Paul. Paul
drops his fork and flees. He has seen this
rage before, unintentional as it is. David

chases Paul down the hall, past the bedroom
where the adult Paul still sits reading the
letter from his dad. Young Paul rushes
apologizing into the bathroom where he is out
of space to run, trapped between the tub and
hamper, he is hollering how sorry he is,
though he doesn't quite grasp what for.

DAVID. (*Cornering his son*.) Little ingrate!
Complain there's not enough when your Grandma
cooks for all of us!

YOUNG PAUL. (*Crying, blubbering*.) I didn't
mean to!

The light goes dark totally as David closes
in on Young Paul, slaps and bawls are heard.

End act 1, scene 1.

Act 1, Scene 2

Light comes up on the gypsy cab, a rusted
out, pieced together car, staged with the
driver coming toward the audience, downstage
and left, though it is closer back to the
background mural as it drives through the
Kentucky countryside with Paul Shannon and
John Harper on opposite sides in the back.
Paul is nearer the audience. A handmade sign
on the driver's door of the country taxi cab
says BIG SANDY TRANSPORT. They ride in
silence a few beats.

JOHN HARPER. (*Looks from the ridge mural he
has been staring out to address Paul, who has
been looking out of his side toward the
audience.*) Airport or clinic?

PAUL. (*A bit slow in response, having
resolved to remain silent throughout this
country ride share transportation.*) Airport.
Back to Philly. Back to work. (*He trails
off a bit, then remembers he has to return
volley.*) You?

JOHN HARPER. Clinic. Two reasons people cab
from Red Knife to Lexington. Airport or
clinic.

PAUL. (*In agreement.*) Airport or clinic.

JOHN HARPER. You ever wonder what this place
looked like before they settled in? I mean
before the trail blazers came through and
built the places and put people around.

Paul nods and tries to give an easy smile, though he is clearly unsure about being drawn into this conversation.

JOHN HARPER.   (*Continuing.*) It's funny, I guess, some places just get settled and then some don't. Take the North pole. That Byrd feller went all the way up there and jabbed our American flag, bless its soul, into snow and ice. But it ain't settled. Can't be. A place that cold and that far away from people. Way I figure it, that old Byrd was just running away. Run so far he made it to the top of the world, maybe. But all the same, he was just running. (Leaning across the seat at Paul.) You running from something or to something, young man?

CAB DRIVER.   (*Pulling over and to a stop.*) University of Kentucky Clinic.

JOHN HARPER. Name's John Harper. Have a good flight. It's good weather for traveling. I hope your family visit was nice. This is my stop.

Paul is stunned at John Harper's turn of conversation and doesn't manage to formulate a reply. John eases himself up and out of the cab and moves gingerly toward the back of the stage at right, then suddenly he turns back before the cab can pull away.

JOHN HARPER. (*Looking into the backseat and talking to Paul again.*) I'm sorry to hear about your father…truth is though, he died a long time ago. Ask your uncle. (*He turns now suddenly in a hurry for his appointment*

and calls again as he moves out of view.)
Just ask your Uncle Hill!

There is a fade to black, then as the lights
rise again, the cab is flipped in the
opposite direction, though Paul still sits to
the side nearest the audience.

CAB DRIVER. I don't care if you want to pay
me to take you back, buddy. You're acting
like it's a big deal for some reason, I was
going to be driving straight back as soon as
I dropped you at the airport anyways. What's
the big deal? It's one-fifty to ride back,
just like it was one-fifty to ride here with
me.

There is a moment or two of silence. Paul
leans forward in the back studying something:
it is the cab driver's placard card fixed on
the dash.

PAUL. (*Now knowing the man's name.*) Hey,
Ron?

CAB DRIVER. (*Turns his head as if to say,
'how in the hell do you know my name?' as
Paul points at the placard. Nods in
understanding.*) Yea?

PAUL. Who was that old man who rode up with
us? Did you notice how he didn't say a word
all the way up here and then got chatty once
we made it?

CAB DRIVER. Well, all I know is Caleb back
at the office said he was a Harper guy.
Papers are back at work. Like I'd tell you

his address and everything anyway, buddy.
That seems like something I shouldn't do.
I'm gonna push it to sixty-five if that's
okay with you?

PAUL.   (*Trying to relax.*) Yea, sure, man.
(*He sits back a few moments, then has to lean
forward again and ask another question.*) Can
you tell me where you picked the guy up at?

CAB DRIVER. I already told you, I really
can't.

The lights fade. End act 1, scene 2.

Act 1, Scene 3

As the light comes up we are back in the
Shannon kitchen where a returned Paul sits
with his grandparents, William and Eve. It
is just twilight though William and Eve are
dressed for bed in blue and pink night shirts
respectively. The Shannons are loving
grandparents to Paul, though are clearly
weary from the day's funeral service and
hosting a small group of friends and family
afterwards.

WILLIAM.   (*Rising*.) Eve, I think it's about
time for bed. This old boy is tired and
hurting in his heart. But right now, more
tired. (*William looks directly now at his
grandson and puts a hand on his shoulder.*)
Pray for us, Paul. Pray that we can sleep.
The last two nights we've only had a couple
hours sleep and it was all nightmares.
Dreams about your dad, when he was healthy
and young. You should have seen him then.
But then me and your grandmother would wake
up and he was gone all over again. It was a
waking nightmare, Paul. Pray we can sleep.

EVE.   (*Following the lead of her husband,
rising*.) Pray for us all, Paul. You get
some sleep, too. You need to rest, baby.
I'm glad you decided to extend your stay
awhile. (*She and William exit down the
hallway to their unseen bedroom past the
bathroom.*)

Paul sits at the table a few bits longer. He
gets up and looks in the refrigerator
absently. He switches off the light as he

exits the kitchen and walks into the bedroom off next to the kitchen. He flops on the bed. He looks at the pill bottles on the nightstand, inspecting the contents of two or three bottles before settling on what he wants. He opens the bottle and takes a handful of pills he then dry swallows.

The lights go down and total darkness lasts a moment or two. When the light comes back up, it is midday. A hulking figure appears behind the 3 slats in the kitchen door. It knocks loudly.

In the bedroom next to the kitchen Paul is fidgeting under the covers at the knocking. He pulls them tighter over his head. When the knocking continues, he jerks the covers off his body. He gets up gingerly but urgently, as one roused from a dream by a phone call trying to answer the phone before the caller hangs up. As he comes out of the bedroom he peers around the corner of the hallway into the kitchen just as the knocking stops. He sees just a chin in the 3 window panes at the top of the door. It does not appear the figure is turning to leave. The knocking resumes.

PAUL.   (*Irritated but trying to not to be.*) Just a minute! (*He crosses the kitchen to the door and opens it. LARRY stands there, hulking, with his childish overalls and crew cut*).

LARRY. (*Giving as friendly a smile as he can. He asks his question as a ten-year-old coming to ask if the neighbor kid can play.*) Is David home?

PAUL. (*Unsure.*) I guess you should step in for a minute. Were you friends with my dad?

LARRY. (*Excited.*) I sure was! (*He claps his two hands together to show a bond.*) I was your daddy's best friend. My name is Larry Fenner.

Paul stands aside and Larry enters the kitchen.

LARRY. Larry Fenner. (*He helps himself to a chair and sits at the kitchen table. As he does so, his knees pop up to the edge of the table.*) You mean your daddy never did say nothing about Larry Fenner? (*At this realization he appears a little hurt.*)

PAUL. (*Deciding on a blunt approach.*) Larry, my father passed away. Just this past week. I'm sorry.

LARRY. (*Drops his head and stares at his meaty hands.*) Your dad, Dave, would put your butt in the sling if he heard you saying it like that. Passed away. (*He looks into the distance of the audience.*) People don't pass away. They're not like a bad smell or campfire smoke. People die and that's the way it is. (*He looks now squarely at Paul, who in enraptured by this beast of a man.*) Anyway, that's what your dad, Dave, used to say. (*Pause.*) I was his best friend.

Larry looks from his spot at the table downstage left, where a fence row and the young boys, Dave, Hill, and Tommy, are gathered. As he does so the spotlight follows his stare and as the young boys at the fence row are fully illuminated the kitchen goes dim with Larry and Paul watching the past.

YOUNG TOMMY. (*Matter of factly, maturely.*) My daddy says it's the hottest August on record for Red Knife.

YOUNG DAVE. That's why we need a good drink.

YOUNG HILL. (*Looking out over the field beyond the fencerow, offstage.*) There's 'ol Larry. I knew his daddy'd have him plowing. Too late in the day for the mule.

YOUNG TOMMY. Boy, I thought my daddy worked me hard. Ain't nobody at school gets worked like Larry by his old man. Using him like a plow horse.

YOUNG DAVE. (*To the field.*) Larry! Get over here man! (*Turning to talk quieter to Hill and Tommy.*) His daddy beats him like a plow horse too. Wonder what they're doing at school right now?

Young Larry ambles up to the fence, much larger than the other boys, though still a peer. He is covered in dirt and sweat, as one plowing a field by hand in the sun would be.

YOUNG DAVE. (*Addressing Larry before Larry even speaks, allowing Larry to go ahead and catch his breath.*) We're taking off. (*Larry starts to climb the fence and Young Dave is the only of the three boys to help Larry, giving Larry a chance to catch his breath.*) Let's go. You have to go. I mean we skipped out on the whole damn day.

YOUNG LARRY (*He brushes the dirt out of his hair, as the other boys react to the swirling dust, he finally speaks.*) You guys better just go on ahead and I'll catch up. Daddy's not bound to let me go much of anywhere today, you know, turning the field and all. (*He nods with his head back toward the field beyond the fence he's already escaped.*)

YOUNG DAVE. (*Gesturing to an imagined porch beyond the imagine field.*) He's asleep, man. Look at him over there slumped in the chair on the porch.

Young Larry leans on the fence row with his forearms and stares in that direction with a look of concession.

YOUNG HILL. (*Interjecting.*) I know you're scared to go. (*Hill steps into the space between his brother Dave and Larry and leans next to Larry on the fence.*) I don't blame you. Ain't none of us know what it's like. I mean we've been whipped some, but nothing like— (*He cuts himself off.*) Anyway, if you don't want to go then you don't have to. We're just saying it would be fun is all.

YOUNG DAVE. (*Liking this line of argument, he perks up and leans on the fence as well, though he's already been facing it to look beyond the field.*) Yea, Hoss, that's the thing. We just don't want to miss out on the fun. Just like Hill said. Se, we ain't told you where we're really heading have we?

Young Tommy has remained back away from the fence row, not interested in trying to persuade Young Larry.

YOUNG LARRY. I figure you're going down to Harper's Tipple to drink some.

YOUNG DAVE. That's right. We're heading up to the Coal Tipple of Drink. Old Harper's.

YOUNG HILL. (*Pulling away from the fence and patting Larry on his forearm causing dust to swirl from his shirt.*) Let's go, Larry. If he wakes up and sees you're gone, we'll take hell for it right along with you, all right?"

YOUNG LARRY. (*He looks up as with exasperation but as he looks down he is friendly, having been talked into going to have fun with his buddies.*) You guys won't get what I'm gonna get, but that's all right. You'll get what you're used to and that's bad enough, I guess. Let's go.

The three boys push away from the railing and walk toward the backstage area. Young Tommy joins these three in a line as they march backstage to the left of the giant ridge mural. They are laughing and joking under their breath as they walk behind the mural.

They emerge on the right side of the mural
and walk down and off stage right. They then
use the small ladder at the front of the
stage to climb up onto the stage and tipple
scaffold set. As the four young boys move
behind the mural and back around, adult Larry
and Paul remain in the kitchen, following the
movement of the boys, looking back to the
mural as the boys pass behind it, then
following the group of boys to the scaffold
set. The boys climb the ladder and reach the
scaffold in the order of Larry, Hill, and
Dave. Tommy struggles coming up the ladder.

YOUNG DAVE. (*As he clears the top of the
ladder to the scaffold, he looks down,
calling back to Tommy.*) Get your tremblin'
ass up here. Look at Larry.

A few seconds pass after Dave clears the
ladder to the scaffold. The three boys on
the scaffold move to the old padlocked metal
ice chest at the right of the scaffold as
Tommy finally clears the ladder and gets onto
the scaffold, walking a bit unsteady.

YOUNG LARRY. (*As if looking in the distance
from this scaffold high up the tipple.*) The
land of milk and honey.

YOUNG DAVE. (*Kneeling at the ice chest with
Hill.*) I got your milk and honey right here.

YOUNG TOMMY. (*A little shaky but wanting
desperately to be part of the gang.*) I
wish't it was winter. (*Trying to sound
grown-up, mimicking his dad perhaps.*) Beer
so cold it'd bust a man's teeth down the

middle. Hot like this means the beer's gonna
be warm as piss.

As Tommy has been doing his best to shoot the
shit like his old man, Dave has started
digging in both pockets.

YOUNG DAVE. (*In a kind of controlled panic,
whispering.*) Shit. Shit!

YOUNG HILL. (*Noticing Dave clearly cannot
find the key to the padlock as Dave digs
around in his pockets.*) Tell me you're just
dealing with a bad case of crabs.

YOUNG LARRY. (*Still looking off into the
distance, not worried as Dave and Hill
clearly grow frustrated*). Crabs! Ha! (*He
sits and dangles his legs off the scaffold.*)

YOUNG HILL. Not those kind of crabs. (*Rolls
his eyes to Tommy and Dave.*)

YOUNG LARRY. What kind? (*He is wildly
dangling his legs now.*)

YOUNG DAVE. (*Turning to look at Larry, who
is wildly dangling his feet.*) You're gonna
fall one of these days doing that. (*To the
entire group.*) We need something to get that
lock off. I gotta plan.

The light goes completely dark on the tipple
scaffold and brightens once again in the
Shannon kitchen at the center of the stage
where the adult Larry and Paul Shannon have
been watching the memory of the young boys
play out. They are broken from their intent

stares in the direction of the scaffold on the stage by the stirring of EVE and WILLIAM SHANNON from their sleep.

EVE SHANNON. (*Shuffling down the hall past the bathroom and the bedroom next to the kitchen, tired, still in her pink pajama shirt having finally slept. Before she gets to the kitchen she calls out.*) Who's in there?

PAUL. (*To Larry at the table where the two have been sitting.*) It's Mamaw. She's been sleeping, you know. She's been real tired.

Larry straightens up in his chair, smooths the front of his bib overalls as if trying to impress.

EVE. (*Coming round the corner to the kitchen, clearly recognizing Larry Fenner, though he is much older. She treats him with great kindness.*) Larry Fenner, Larry Fenner, where have you been? (*She has brightened as best she can, despite being a grieving mother.*) Would you like me to cook you something? (*She doesn't wait for an answer, and grabs a couple of things from the fridge on the way to the stove. She uses a large cast iron already on the stove, and goes about the business of pancake making.*)

LARRY. I remember your big pots of spaghetti. David called 'em gangster meals. Just like in the gangster movies, a big pot of spaghetti and garlic bread to last a month!

EVE. (*Not turning back, continuing to cook. Joking despite her grief.*) A month heck! You boys would eat it all up! Hotcakes will have to do for now. I know it's not morning anymore but some of us have been sleeping the rough off today. (*Because she cannot shake her motherly mannerism, she adds the advice a bit sing-songy*) We all need a little nourishment.

LARRY. (*Suddenly rising from the table, gracefully in a way, and silently moving across the room, nestling behind Eve Shannon at the stove. He wraps his huge arms around her from behind and gives her an embracing hug. Eve Shannon and Paul are startled first by this grip, but Eve Shannon welcomes the embrace when she realizes what it is and Paul relaxes. We hear steps coming down the hall.*) I'm sorry about my friend Dave and your boy Dave.

William Shannon appears in the kitchen as Larry gives a final squeeze then moves back to his seat at the kitchen table.

WILLIAM. (*Clearly joking.*) Ain't but one man suppose to wrap his arms around my wife, Larry Fenner, and that's me.

Paul rises and walks to meet his grandfather. He hugs William.

WILLIAM. (*Still joking.*) Hey, Paul. What'd you drag in with you here? Today's Tuesday. We're supposed to take garbage out on Tuesdays, not bring it in.

Larry gets this is joking, but still has an air of embarrassment. He rises and offers his hand as William Shannon comes to the table. William Shannon accepts his hand, and while he is joking and warm, he has something skeptical in his expression about the appearance of his dead son's old friend.

WILLIAM. (*Moving now towards his wife at the stove.*) What've we got cooking here, guys? (*He rubs his wife's back lovingly as he reaches the stove.*)

LARRY. I am sorry about your boy. It hurts me, too, Mr. Shannon. I was Dave's best friend.

WILLIAM. (*Turns from his wife and gives something like a glare of resentment, though tries to keep a veneer of warmth.*) Yes, friends, David could have used more friends, but none as much as here lately. It seems the ones he did have just had other things to do for the past twenty years. (*He throws his arms up in the air, signifying all the other things there must have been to do.*) Where exactly have you been all this time, Larry? Why haven't you came to see David or Eve or me? Lord knows we kept you like our on while your daddy… (*He trails off, catching his tongue with some effort. He realizes he is on the verge of berating and decides to cool it.*) Anyway, I suppose it's good to see you now. Can you still put down a stack of hotcakes a foot high?

Larry nods absently. He is picking at his elbow and his eyes are scanning the table

cloth as Paul and William stare at Larry.
Eve continues cooking. Larry jerks a bit in
his seat, as if uncontrollably, then switches
from picking his elbow to give a few
scratches down the length of his calf. He
jerks again as he does so, then murmurs to
himself under his breath. Something is
clearly not okay with Larry and his little
ticks.

WILLIAM. (*Trying to be more concerned than
judgmental but both come out.*) What in the
world are you doing?

LARRY. (*Stops fidgeting, but still fixes his
gaze on the tablecloth. His voice is a bit
far away.*) Huh?

WLLIAM. I said are you all right?

PAUL. (*Breaking in, wanting to relieve
whatever tension this is.*) Ah, he's just
hungry, and the tough news sinking in. (*As he
says this, he is staring to William as if he
is quite uncertain about what is actually
happening.*)

William starts to speak, but Eve has just
finished the stack and turns around ready to
serve, not fully aware of the mini drama
playing out with Larry. She places a stack
of pancakes on a big plate in the middle of
the table.

EVE. Are we ready to eat?

LARRY. (*Leaning forward a bit suspicious of
the stack.*) Do these have crabs in them?

EVE. What?

LARRY. (*Matter of factly but still off in his head somewhere else.*) Can I catch crabs off these? You know, jumping crabs?

Lights go down.

End act 1, scene 3.

Act 1, Scene 4

The light comes up in the bedroom next to the
kitchen. It is just daylight, early morning.
Young Paul wakes in the little trundle bed
perpendicular to David's bed. He lifts a wet
sheet. He is worried as he has wet the bed.
He stands and observes his wet pajama front.
As he turns the audience sees he is quite wet
on the backside too. Paul looks back to see
his dad has already gotten out of bed. His
movements are nervous as he strips the fitted
and flat sheet off his little bed. He balls
them and leaves them on the bed intending to
go to the bathroom and clean himself off
first. He goes into the hall and turns into
the bathroom. To his startled surprise, his
dad is sitting on the toilet with a textbook.
He is scared to death thinking what his
father will do when he sees he has wet the
bed again. David Shannon though doesn't
leave his own thoughts at first to see what
his son has done. The absence of the
expected reactions of trying to shut the door
back or yelling about the wet sheets makes
Young Paul more nervous.

DAVID. (*Still looking at the book, having
only glanced at his son.*) I believe if I'd
had a good teacher in high school I could
have learned this. It's hard trying to teach
yourself. (*He breaks off and raises his head
and sees Paul standing nervously in the
doorway with his wet pajamas. He still does
not explode as with the mashed potatoes.*)
What the hell? (*He stands up, as he was not
using the toilet, simply sitting on its lid
to have a quiet place to read.*) Did you piss

yourself just now? Why'd you do that? Why didn't you tell me you needed the bathroom?

Paul doesn't say anything as he is quite uncertain of how to answer the question.

DAVID. Well, don't just stand there. Close the door and I'll get out of here so you can clean yourself up. Jesus Christ.

The two exchange positions, Paul going into the bathroom and David coming out with his book. David goes into the bedroom and sees the pile of sheets on his son's bed. He comes back to the hallway just as Young Paul opens the bathroom door, now a big towel covering his body and his pajamas in a wet ball.

YOUNG PAUL. (*Knowing his dad has now seen the sheets too. He is defeated.*) I peed the bed. I pee the bed sometimes.

DAVID. (*Genuinely confused.*) You wet the bed sometimes? (*Seeing how ashamed his son is, David tries to make it better, but still takes a shot at his ex-wife.*) Not a problem. How long had your mom known about this? It doesn't matter, I know what to do. Get your covers and sheets. (*He nods in the direction of the bedroom from where they stand between the bathroom and bedroom.*) I'll show you how to put them and your pajamas in the wash and turn on the machine. That way if this happens again, you can take care of it and your grandmother doesn't have to clean up after you.

YOUNG PAUL. (*Relieved his father is not angry, but not untimid.*) Okay.

Paul goes to get the sheets from the bed, adds them to the pajama pile he carries, and joins his father back in front of the bathroom. They disappear stage left together toward the laundry room.

END ACT 1

Act 2, Scene 1

The lights come up on the Act 2 set, with
Uncle Hill's trailer house set on
cinderblocks in the middle of the stage, open
to the audience. Signs surround the trailer
house, including "Hillman's Car & Truck
Parts" and "Elect Shannon," in reference to
some unknown local election of the past. The
signs are faded and look like they have been
scrawled by an eight-year-old. Paul stands
behind the door of the trailer which faces
the backstage mural. The audience, seeing
through the open wall of the trailer sees
Hill in his recliner reading. The trailer is
quite messy, full of books and papers and
what-nots. When Paul knocks, Hill rises as
if angry to be disturbed. When he sees it is
his nephew returned though he is pleasantly
surprised, expecting Paul had already
returned to Philly.

UNCLE HILL. Hey, long time no see. You
ain't been gone but a day or so. What's got
you back here?

PAUL. About the craziest thing you can
imagine has me back here. (*He looks around
at his Uncle's mess. He jokes.*) Did I ever
tell you that you live in a dump?

UNCLE HILL. (*Returning to his recliner. As
he sits he clears the chair just near him for
Paul. He gestures for Paul to sit, but Paul
waves him off, preferring in his antsy state
to walk around and look at his uncle's
affects.*) Yea, you've mentioned it. So you
say your mom's hanging in there huh?

PAUL.   Yeah she's up north.   Moved about two years ago to be closer to me on the East Coast.   (*He continues to look around at books, photos, clips of newspaper.*)

UNCLE HILL.   See, that's what I'm talking about.   Mary never did nothing that wasn't with you in mind.   (*Paul continues looking around at this and that.   Hill realizes that Paul doesn't want to engage the topic of his mother anymore and isn't planning on replying to the compliment Hill is trying to give Paul's mom.*)   What'd the letter say?

PAUL. (*He looks back over his shoulder from his casual rummaging of printed material.*) You know, the same stuff.   You know how Dad was.

UNCLE HILL.   Was.   Yep.   Man it's crazy to say was.   I miss him a lot, Paul.

PAUL. (*Turning fully and guffawing some.*) You gotta be kidding me, seriously kidding me. You don't have to say that on my account. (*Paul sees Hill is a bit hurt, and really is just trying to kind to his nephew here.*) Well, in the spirit of small talk, how's it going?

UNCLE HILL. It's going.   (*He rubs the stubble on his chin, and makes a few attempts at getting the hair to flatten on his head.*) You read the note I gave you at the funeral home, you say? The letter?   (*He has decided to be persistent in talking about his dead brother, Paul's dead father.*)

PAUL. Yeah.

UNCLE HILL. I didn't read it, by the way. I
figured that was something between you and
Dave. Between you and your daddy. I don't
know how much money was in that jar either.
Didn't count it.

PAUL. I appreciate you bringing it by the
house for me. Why'd you clear outta the
funeral so fast. You didn't say bye, just
hopped in that old S-10 and mufflered outta
there.

UNCLE HILL. (*Now the object of defense in
the conversation.*) Well, I would've. But
you know how fake those things get, and how
the fake can make a body ill. I figure I
hurt just as bad here as there and here I've
got my own peace of mind to comfort me. But
then, I ramble. I figured you'd be gone by
now.

PAUL. (*Rubbing his own chin stubble.*) Yeah,
I know. Listen, I had something really
strange happen when I was going to Lexington.
I'm just going to tell you. It's why I came
back.

UNCLE HILL. (*Trying to relax back in his
chair at this interesting twist, but trying
to remain attentive, there for his nephew.*)
I'm all ears, as they say.

PAUL. (*Being sly, trying to gauge the
reaction.*) I shared a cab with John Harper.

UNCLE HILL.   (*Perplexed*.) John Harper?

PAUL.   Yeah, John Harper. Says I'm supposed
to ask my Uncle Hill something.

UNCLE HILL.   'John Harper' he said his name
was?

PAUL.   Yes, John Harper. That's what he
said.   And he knows you and he knew my dad
had died.   But said Dad really died long ago
someway.   He knew us.   Acted like he knew
everything about the Shannons there was to
know.

UNCLE HILL.   Well not the everything… (*Hill
catches himself as he has let too much go.
He then relents*.)   Not really even close,
truth be told.   (*He sighs, knowing he might
as well connect the dots as Paul seeks*.)   Dad
came by, said Larry's come by.

PAUL.   (*Realizing Uncle Hill is going to
connect the dots*.) Yea. He did. I don't think
he knew about dad dying.   I think he was just
visiting.

UNCLE HILL.   I haven't talked to Larry since
junior high, well the summer before we
started high school.   Did anyone even tell
you about Harper's Tipple?

Paul shakes his head.

UNCLE HILL.   John Harper, the John Harper I
knew was George Harper's boy. Though I
thought he was long dead or moved off.   The
Harpers were incredibly wealthy.   Owned coal

mines all over Mays County. Even had one on
the Harper property after they found a good
seam of coal there, which was some kind of
mineral miracle, truth be told. (*Adopting
his lawyerly affectation.*) Thus, the big
tipple on the Harper property.

PAUL. What does this have to do with Larry?

UNCLE HILL. What happened is I ran away,
Paul. But then, I'm good at that, or so
people say.

PAUL. What's that mean you 'ran away'?

UNCLE HILL. (*He's starting to drift.*) Oh ask
people, they'll tell you. How I abandoned a
good profession in law, lots of money and
power, a good life. How I sit out here outta
town surrounded by junk cars in this old
trailer. I ran away from life. I ran away
from Harper's that day. It's the thing I'm
good at.

PAUL. Jesus, Uncle Hill. What about
Harper's Tipple?

UNCLE HILL. Well, it was really something
your dad shoulda told you about.

PAUL. He can't now.

UNCLE HILL. No, no I don't guess he can.
(*Hill stands up and heads to rummage in the
bottom of a cabinet below a book shelf. He
manages to pull out an old album.*) I should
have brought this out for you a long time
ago, I guess. But I just didn't see any

reason for it. Plus, I wasn't sure your daddy hadn't told you, or somebody else for that matter. There was always the chance of that. (*He pauses, composing himself, ashamed of his sin of silence.*) Either way, there it is. (*He hands the mustard colored album to Paul who takes it and finally sits in the chair Hill cleared for him earlier. At this, Hill re-sits in his chair. When Paul opens to the first page, Hill supplements.*) You know who that is, don't you?

PAUL. Dad?

UNCLE HILL. Yep. Junior high. That was the year before the acne got hold of him. Damn that was bad. We hadn't even heard of laser surgery and here Dave was having it done on his face. Daddy thought they had poisoned him. Thought it had changed him because of how different he was later on.

PAUL. (*Not interested in the laser surgery story, interested in the contents of the album and having it explained.*) Why was his junior high picture in the paper?

UNCLE HILL. Thing is, what you're about to see…hell, Paul, what you're about to see is what you're about to see, I guess. That's all. We found it under Dave's mattress. Look at it when you're ready. I'll be outside. Take as long as you want. (*He stands and exits the door down to his yard out of sight.*)

PAUL. (*Watches his uncle exit, then slowly turns to the next page. He pulls out a*

*couple of loose, brittle newspaper clippings
and begins to read aloud.)* Search for
missing boy continues. Officials, family
fear the worst. David Shannon has been
missing for three days… (*Paul trails off and
reads the story silently a few moments. He
switches to another clipping he holds and
reads aloud.*) Red Knife boy found.
Officials confirmed that Dave Shannon, a boy
missing several days, has been found and
returned to his family. Shannon's parents
did not comment on the incident specifically,
except to say they were pleased to have him
home, and that he was recovering well, having
suffered much physical strain during the
ordeal. However, local friends of the Red
Knife Junior High student, particularly those
who were with him the day he disappeared,
spoke briefly with gathered press shortly
after the youth was discovered. One of
those, David Shannon's brother, Hillman
Shannon, said that he and his brother had
been at Harper's Tipple with friends the day
David Shannon went missing. Faculty at the
school confirmed that David Shannon, Hillman
Shannon and Thomas Spencer, of Pratt Hill
Road, had apparently left school grounds
without permission that day, having been
marked as truant from their teachers.
According to school records, only two other
students were absent on the day Shannon went
missing, one, Larry Fenner, whom Principal
Ward reports has a history of absenteeism.
Fenner was not available for comment. With
very few clues as to exactly how Shannon went
missing, one thing authorities have had
little trouble in understanding, however, is
where David Shannon was eventually found.

The particulars of that scene have not yet
been released to the press, but sources close
to the family have said the 12-year-old was
nearly starved when found and had suffered
from exhaustion, apparent shock and
dehydration… (He trails off again as the
lights dim.)

End act 2, scene 1.

Act 2, Scene 2

The spotlight comes up again on the partial
tipple and scaffold step at the edge of
downstage right. The boys are there as
before, Young Larry dangling his legs, Dave
and Hill and Tommy gathered round the locked
metal ice chest.

YOUNG DAVE. I have a plan.

YOUNG TOMMY. (*In mockery.*) You have a plan.

Dave walks toward Larry, and pretends to push
him off in play, before sitting down next to
Larry.

YOUNG DAVE. (*Pointing down to the ground far
below.*) Can you see that shining in the sun
down there on that pile of coal, Larry?
(*Everyone strains to see what Dave was
pointing out. Young Dave is really just
goofing, and talks almost like a car salesman
here.*) I do believe that shining thing way
down there at the base of the tipple is a
crowbar. Would definitely stand in quite
nicely to pop this lock off, Master lock or
not.

Young Larry, silently, stands and slumps
toward the top of the ladder, clearly
obeying.

YOUNG DAVE. (*Catching Larry's shoulder,
continuing his joke.*) Now I appreciate that
gesture, Hoss, we all do, but they ain't a
bit a use in you climbing all the way back
down that thing when all you need to is go

off this side over here, plop down in that
nice soft coal left at the bottom, then bring
that sucker right on up. That pile is easy
twenty, twenty-five feet high, and when it
sits like that for so long it breaks down and
gets softer, weathered, that kind of thing.

YOUNG HILL. What? That's idiotic.

YOUNG DAVE. (*Intent on getting Larry's and
Tommy's goats.*) Don't give me that, Hill.
You know and I know—hell maybe even Tommy
knows—that coal, the way it's laying like
that is just as soft as a stack of dish rags.
It ain't gonna hurt Larry. Besides we all
know too that he's just about the bravest and
toughest guy in the bunch. You might not
want to admit it, but it's true just the
same. (*Young Dave goes full pitch man, a
carnival barker throwing fastballs.*) Who
else would stand up at the Strand and sing
"The Old Gray Mule" with everybody there
chomping on popcorn and waiting for the show?
Who here would jump from the top of Clark's
Tunnel into the back of a moving coal gon-
doh-la? We had to lift Dad's Chrysler and
drive halfway across the state just to pick
him up! And what was he doing when we picked
him up? (*Tommy shakes his head, his eyes
getting wider with every detail. Hill is no
longer paying attention to his brother's
show. Larry acts shy at the shower of false
praise.*) He was taking bets with them locals
on how many hot peppers he could eat in five
minutes. He got through two and half jars
with time to spare! Remember, Hill? We used
the money for gas on the way back. (*Hill
nods reflexively but continues to look away.*)

So then tell me who else here is right for
this job, this feat that will stand as a
legend in this town? Nobody else, right?

YOUNG HILL. (*In admonishment of his brother's
silliness, refusing to be the captive
audience to his brother's tales Tommy and
Larry were.*) Why don't you go down and get
something to open the chest with?

YOUNG DAVE. (*Disappointed his brother will
not go along.*) Forget it then! I'll do it.

Dave turns and is about to head down the
ladder when a loose section of the catwalk
shifts beneath his feet, and he stumbles. As
he does, the other boys shake and try to gain
balance at the now swinging scaffold. Tommy
and Hill regain balance. Larry, like a
stone, falls forward and drops off the
scaffold, almost like he went with the fall
rather than trying to resist it, dropping off
the front of the stage.

YOUNG TOMMY. Christ almighty!

Lights dim. End act 2, scene 2.

Act 2, Scene 3

The lights rise and we hear the strains and
grunts of Young Dave trying to drag the
hulking Young Larry. They emerge at left of
the big mural from backstage and move past
the Fenner shed and come to the Fenner porch.
Joe Fenner is leaned at his porch rail as the
boys approach. He does not fly off the porch
as a concerned father seeing a mangled son
should, but instead calls down as the two
boys approach.

JOE FENNER. (*Equal parts concern and anger.*)
Goddamn! Larry.

YOUNG DAVE. (*Struggling beneath the weight of
his hurt friend.*) He's hurt, Mr. Fenner.
(*He manages to get Larry to the porch steps.
Joe meets him there and takes Larry's limp
and broken body from Dave and lays Larry on
the porch. He turns back to Dave with great
anger.*) Mr. Fenner, Larry fell off the
tipple out at—(*Joe punches Dave and Dave
knocks right out.*)

JOE FENNER. (*Calling into the house.*)
Clara, come out here and get this boy.
Splint up his legs. He's broke 'em all to
shit. Maybe his hips too. (*Leaving his
injured son on the porch, throws Young Dave
over his shoulder and marches him back to the
shed. He tosses Dave into the shed through
the door on the side.*) In you go you little
prick! (*Joe slams the door and secures it
shut with a board.*)

YOUNG DAVE. (*Stirs to his senses. He gets to his feet and beats on the door. Then he beats around all the walls, including the imagined one the audience sees through.*)
Hey! Lemme outta here! Hey! Hey! Hey!
Hey, let me out! (*He falls to his knees. In the foreground on the porch, Joe and the now appeared Clara gather and drag their son inside as best they can.*) Please let me out!
Larry needs to go to the hospital! Larry's legs are gone! Larry needs legs! (*He collapses in the dirt floor of the shed crying.*)

The lights dim and rise again, daylight having changed, Young Dave having collapsed in exhaustion and despair and slept. A knock and a low whisper as the lights are out.

CLARA FENNER.   (*Whispering.*) Dave.

The lights come up and we see Clara is at the door at the side of the shed, whispering through the crack to Young Dave who is awakening. When he gathers himself he stands, and then lunges at the door with his shoulder trying to pop it open, to no affect.

CLARA FENNER.   (*Whispering but louder now.*)
Shhh, now be quiet, little Shannon. I can't let you outta there, boy. Don't you understand that? My boy's a laying in there with his legs needing chopped off and I can't take him to no hospital. Joe won't allow it.
Just wanted you to know about Larry. (*She pauses a beat. There is something like sympathy in her voice, yet at the same time she is as cruel as her husband.*) Joe's mean,

but you deserve this, you know that. You
deserve whatever evil he pushes on you,
Little Shannon.

As if on cue, Joe Fenner comes out onto the
porch and looks to the shed where Clara is
talking through the door to Dave. He walks
off the porch and too the shed, beginning to
talk before he reaches the door alongside
Clara.

JOE FENNER. Heya there, boy! I got this
board over the door here and you ain't
gettin' out. You hear me? I'm keeping you,
boy. I'm gonna take your legs because you
took my boy's legs. He told me what
happened. Said you boys put him up to
dropping off that fucking tipple out at
Harper's. You gonna pay for that. You gonna
pay hard. The hardesssst. (*At the last sound
of this last word his voice slides into a
snake's hiss.*) You think we might take him
someplace, to the doctor's, leaving you here
on your own in this hot old shed without
water and food and you can try to make your
move. You got another thing coming, Shannon.
We ain't going nowhere. We're going to stay
right here. She's gonna take care of him.
(*He hooked his thumb at his wife even though
Dave can't see him talking.*) And I'm gonna
take care of you.

Young Dave makes no reply, simply collapsing
at the back wall of the shed under the shelf
with the jar and cans.

JOE FENNER. (*Realizing the boy isn't going
to reply.*) Tell you what, I'm gonna step

over here and throw this old shed latch and I
want you to try to jump out of there. I'm
gonna leave the door open so you do that very
thing, cuz then I'm gonna kill you quick.
That's what she says I should do. (*At this he
hooks his thumb at his wife again.*) So you
just take a run for it when I go over there
if you want. I'll kill you quick and then
she'll be satisfied. (*He puts his mouth
right up to the door to be heard, for
emphasis.*) You don't take a run for it when I
leave this door open, then I'm gonna make it
slow and she won't like it. And if Momma's
not happy ain't nobody happy. (*He waits
again for some reply, but gets nothing as
Young Dave is too terrified.*) Naw, I guess
I'll just leave her locked. I'd like it to
be good and slow. Yes, that'll work just
fine. Just fine I think.

END ACT 2

Act 3, Scene 1

As the light comes up we are inside the Fenner household, three rooms of which are now made the center point of the stage, where the Shannon house was in Act 1. In fact, the Fenner house should look similar in color and scheme, though it is messier and more dilapidated than the maintained Shannon home. Instead of the door toward backstage opening into a kitchen as with the Shannon household, the door opens into a living room with a disheveled couch. Clara lays awake in bed in the bedroom next to the living room. There is a window to the outside in this bedroom, same as the Shannon house bedroom. Young Larry is stashed in a back bedroom somewhere out of sight. The shed remains in place in the background, "out behind the house." It should rotate to accommodate the perspective shift from seeing the porch and shed. Its door would now face the backstage area and its shelf with the Mason jar of green beans and cans is now on the left wall, while the audience side wall remains open. Young Dave remains in the shed while we see the action inside the house, occasionally stirring to get more comfortable or listen for noises.

JOE FENNER. (*Entering the bedroom, having checked on Larry, addressing Clara matter of factly, still no veil of actual fatherly concern.*) I'm gonna have to take the boy to the hospital. Something ain't right with the splintin' and I know you'd want me to take him anyway if you get another look at his legs.

Clara sits up and swings both legs over the side of the bed. She pulls her hair back as an afterthought, grabbing a plastic clamp off the night stand to do so. Leaning over, she pulls back the curtain to eyeball the shed.

CLARA FENNER. (*Staring toward the shed through the window, matter of fact in her tone.*) I wanted you to take him soon as he got here.

JOE FENNER. (*Ignoring the criticism.*) You'll have to watch close while I'm gone. I know it's what that boy's been waiting on out there. For us to leave so he can bust through that shit shack.

CLARA FENNER. (*Standing and putting a ratty robe from the floor on over her ratty sleeping shirt.*) You go on and take Larry to the doctor. Everything'll be okay here.

JOE FENNER. (*Stone faced, serious, demanding.*) Don't let that boy out. You hear me?

CLARA FENNER. You think I lost my mind in my sleep last night? I ain't lettin' him go nowehere.

JOE FENNER. You goddamn right you ain't lettin' him go nowhere. You goddamn right.

The lights dim. End act 3, scene 1.

Act 3, Scene 2

The lights come up as Clara reaches the doorway out onto the porch in the living room. She goes out the back of the house and around to the shed door, which faces backstage. There Young Dave is stretched out on the dirt. As Dave hears Clara moving toward the shed, he starts to cower into the corner. Clara opens the door and looks down at the scared child.

CLARA FENNER. (*Holding the door open.*) Com'on. (*She goes into the shed and grabs Dave by the arm and picks him up.*) Com'on honey. Right now we're goin' in the house. Me and you are about to have some big fun.

Clara marches Dave across the stage, back to the door and into the living room. She plops him down on the couch. They stare at each other a few moments, Young Dave unsure of the intention here.

YOUNG DAVE. (*Finally speaking up.*) Can I have something to eat? (*Clara sits next to Dave on the couch now, lascivious.*) Can I have something to eat? (*Clara rubs her leg against Dave's and shakes her head no. Dave whispers his next question.*) Can I go home?

CLARA FENNER. (*Entitled now in her actions with the boy.*) No. You can't go home. But you can have something to eat. (*She lifts her sleeping shirt up to her knees while gathering the back of David's head with the other hand. She shoves him down in between*

her thighs.) You know what to do with
something like that?

Young Dave struggles away, and overcome by
his pain and hunger and disgust of Clara
Fenner, he vomits over the back of the couch.

CLARA FENNER. Jesus! Look what you did you
little shit! (*She lets Young Dave finish and
return to facing her.*) We'll take care of
that later.

Clara Fenner grabs the back of his head again
and pulls him again to her thighs. Young
Dave gags and suffocates on her crotch as the
lights go dim. We have a couple of moments
of darkness and as the lights rise Clara and
Dave have moved to the bedroom where she
busies herself redressing. Young Dave sits
on the bed as he pulls his shirt on.

CLARA FENNER. Com'on. Let's get you back
out there.

She marches him out of the bedroom, through
the living room, out the door, and toward the
shed. As she gets him close to the shed she
spins the boy toward her and grabs his
crotch.

CLARA FENNER. See there, you little shit. I
feel you. You liked it all along. (*She puts
her other finger under his chin, raising his
eyes to hers.*) You breathe a word and you
know he'll kill you, don't you? You know
better to say anything, cuz he'll kill you
and make it hurt. See, I know that's what
you're thinking, he'll kill me anyway, but

not like that he wouldn't. You see, this'll
be me and your little secret, huh. Little
secret. You tell him, he'll skin you like an
old hog. We'll eat you up just like a hog so
nobody ever finds anything. We'll grind the
bones and dust 'em across that piss poor
field out there. (*Dave leans forward in
orgasm, unable to help himself. At this
Clara smiles and laughs.*) We are going to
have so much fun, me and you. You just wait
and see, little Shannon. (*She wiggles her
shoulders in mock.*) My little Shannon.

Before he fully comes back to himself, Clara
shoves Young Dave back into the shed. He
falls all the way into the wall with the
shelf. The Mason jar falls in the dirt.
Noticing it for the first time in the brief
light let into the shed by the open door
before Clara slams and seals it, he grabs the
jar off the dirt floor. Seeing it full of
green beans he opens it and begins to
greedily eat the string beans, trying
desperately to assuage his hunger and
sickness. Light fades.

End act 3, scene 2.

Act 3, Scene 3

The light comes up and Joe Fenner is
addressing his wife who sits on the couch.
He has returned from the hospital. Clara
now wears a pale yellow flower-print dress of
thin fabric.

JOE FENNER. The cops came by. They said
they'd been meaning to come out here but seen
me come into town. They know the Shannon boy
was with Larry last and they're hunting him.
I kept sayin' I hadn't seen him, but they was
damn curious, especially about how Larry got
hurt.

CLARA FENNER. What'd you tell them?

JOE FENNER. I said he fell off a bluff
goofing off somewheres and not paying
attention. Said he hadn't said nothing about
the missing Shannon kid before that. I
handled it smart.

CLARA FENNER. You going to let him go?

JOE FENNER. Goddamnit I ain't got no choice.
(*He goes out the door of the living room and
behind the house set to the shed. He throws
it open. Dave is lying in the corner near
the empty Mason jar, crying quietly.*) Come
on! Sonofabitch.

YOUNG DAVE. Sorry?

JOE FENNER. You 'bout to go. I'm gonna take
you out to the tracks on Elm Branch and gonna
let you out. I'm gonna call the goddamn

newspaper first and tell them I saw that missing fuckin' Shannon boy out there on the tracks at Elm Branch. (*He pulls Dave up to his feet.*) You gettin' this? You'll want to remember everything from now until you get back home real clear, cuz it's real important. If word gets out about what's happened here, about you being here even, I don't think I need to tell you what will happen.

Young Dave oddly pulls away, as if not understanding and insisting on collecting the empty Mason jar. Joe Fenner lets the boy grab the jar, absent in his own insistence that the boy come to and understand what's happening.

JOE FENNER. You better understand me boy. (*He leans right into Young Dave's face, nose to nose.*) I'm lettin' you go. But what I probably ought to do is kill you. (*He scratches his chin as if rethinking his plan.*) Naw, I guess I can't kill you. But that's what I'd do if I knew I could. Let's go.

YOUNG DAVE. (*Clutching the jar.*) Magic beans.

JOE FENNER. What'd you say? (*Young Dave does not reply.*) Look at me! Look at me! (*Young Dave does not react, just hugs the empty Mason jar. Suddenly Joe explodes again.*) You cripplin' fuck! (*Joe begins to violently smack Young Dave.*) This shed nice and comfy boy! I done my time in this shit hole. Same as Larry has done, same as you,

and done it hard. (*He pants, realizing he
has lost control of himself again, deciding
he is going to kill the little Shannon boy
after all. He shoves the boy down.*) But your
time's done now. Yes, yes, yes, I think I'm
gonna kill you, you little prick.

Joe Fenner lets out a rage of a yell, a yell
that includes the hatred of his whole
miserable life. He is blind with anger. He
charges at Young Dave who is still clutching
the Mason jar. He lunges and his yell is cut
in half as Young Dave swings the jar with
might. He strikes Joe Fenner across the
bridge of the nose and Joe Fenner falls face
first in the dirt. Before Joe Fenner can
come to, Young Dave is on top of him. He
relentlessly beats Joe's head with the Mason
jar, past his own exhaustion. As he beats
Joe Fenner to death, Joe Fenner is now silent
and Young Dave is grunting with each stroke.
The lights fade.

End act 3, scene 3.

Act 3, Scene 4

The lights come up on an even more run down
version of the Fenner household. It has
become beyond filthy and dilapidated and is
now disgusting, Larry having lived there on
his own for years now. The shed is full of
junk, and like the house, also more
weathered. There is a knock on the door.
Paul is wondering around the stage area,
holding the Mason jar of money and letter his
father left him. He moves as if looking
around the house and at the shed. He goes to
the shed and opens the door and examines its
contents, cradling his Mason jar all the
while. Suddenly we hear branches and dry
leaves breaking. Appearing from beyond the
shed, backstage, comes Larry Fenner and
clobbers Paul with a board in the head as
Paul turns his attention from the contents of
the shed. The lights dim. When they rise
again, Paul is tied to the bed in the Fenner
household. Larry Fenner sits in a chair in
the room wearing a pale yellow flower-print
dress of thin fabric. He is barefoot and the
dress stops at his kneecaps. He has a cane.
When Larry notices Paul stirring, he
addresses his captive.

LARRY FENNER. (*His voice is now low and full*
of hatred.) Paul Shannon. (*He stands from*
his chair and walks with the cane.) Paul
Shaaaaaaaaaannon. (*Instead of going to Paul*
in the bed, he leans over and grabs a pistol
from the dresser top.)

PAUL. (*In a panic.*) Jesus, Larry, Jesus
Christ, Larry! (*Larry ignores him and, having*

collected the pistol, stalks back and sits in the chair.) What're you doing Larry?!? Larry?!? *(Larry stands, oddly letting the gun clatter to the floor, raises the cane above his head, and begins to beat Paul's legs with the cane. Paul can only lay back and take it, crying in pain.)*

LARRY FENNER. *(Suddenly stops his attack, sits down, gathering the gun, and switches back to his friendly voice, the one he'd had in the Shannon household.)* Have a look here, Paul Shannon. (He *pulls the dress up with the hand holding the gun, revealing large scarring on his thighs.)*

PAUL. *(Sobbing in pain.)* Please, Larry! Oh god, oh god!

LARRY FENNER. *(Letting the dress fall and standing with the gun. Mocks.)* Please, Larry! (He *points the gun at Paul, and Paul shakes in fear. Suddenly, he points the gun at himself and holds it there a beat. He drops the gun to his side.)* There's gonna be a day, Paul Shannon, when you'll be over this and done with it.

PAUL. *(Suddenly lucid though still with sobs of pain.)* I don't think so, Larry. I don't think so.

LARRY FENNER. No, no. You will. That's the way it's supposed to work. Time is supposed to heal wounds. (He *pulls the gun suddenly to his head again and fires as the lights go black.)*

End act 3, scene 4.

Epilogue

The spotlight appears on Paul and his Uncle
Hill at David Shannon's grave. Paul has the
legal pad letter in the Mason jar, now
emptied of the money. A shovel is next to
the headstone, a small hole having already
been dug. Paul stoops and puts the jar with
the letter into the hole next to the
headstone. He covers it with the dirt pile
using his foot and the shovel.

PAUL SHANNON. (*Stepping back, putting the
shovel on his shoulder, a weapon resting. He
speaks as if to his Uncle, but to himself
just as much.*) He's gone. What happens
next?

UNCLE HILL. (*Resigned to the fate of the
living.*) Tomorrow. Tomorrow comes next.

END PLAY.

<u>Rafting</u>

a ten-minute play,
in supplement to
<u>The Mason Jar</u>

(adapted from the
novel <u>Dysphoria</u>
by Sheldon Lee Compton)

Characters

<u>David Shannon:</u> late 30s; wears old jeans with retro Nike runners and a loose button up plaid, as worn as his jeans; his manner is braced, as if against a wind not blowing, even when he is trying to be kind with his son
<u>Paul Shannon:</u> 8 or 9 or 10; wears jeans and modern sneakers with a loudly colored print t-shirt; generally apprehensive in dealing with his dad, careful not to set him off

A Note on Staging and Production

Can be performed in spotlight with only the deflated raft as a prop, though may also stage a hillside coming down to a river a bank in mural or construction. The action takes place on the bank of the river, the pickup presumably parked up on the hill behind our actors, the river running between actors and audience. Can be used as a spotlighted dialogue while scene changes take place between act breaks of <u>The Mason Jar.</u>

Scene

At rise, our father and son, David and Paul,
are walking up to the river, having just
descended the hill, David caring a folded,
deflated raft, fresh out of its box. David
walks ahead with confidence, Paul lags a step
or two, looking to his dad and the river,
apprehensive about the planned adventure.

PAUL. (*Wishing to say the right thing, he
instead says the first thing that pops into
his mind when he looks out to the other
rafters on the river.*) Whoa, they got some
big rafts.

DAVID. (*Not caring to notice, looking for a
good flat spot to kneel and unfold the raft
to inflate it.*) Well, they got lots of people
in the raft. We just got us here. (*He finds
his desired surface and drops the deflated
raft. He kneels beside it to get to work.*)

PAUL. (*Agreeing but uncertain.*) Yea. (*He sits
on the river bank near his kneeling father
and pulls his knees to his chin to watch.*)

Paul watches as his dad squats beside him,
bent over the raft, inhaling then exhaling in
large bursts into the little clear nipple.
The raft hardly moves, expanding only subtly,
then dying again, flat and collapsed.

PAUL. Are you sure it's gonna work?

DAVID. (*Continuing his fruitless labors all
the while. Talking between inhales and
exhales.*) Yea it'll work. It's brand new

outta the box. You saw. Paid twenty bucks at the truck stop.

PAUL. (*Timid, but as a child he can't help but vocalize his anxieties, his questions.*) Yea, just the box was old and dusty and at the bottom of a shelf.

DAVID. (*Continuing his fruitless labors all the while. Talking between inhales and exhales.*) But the raft is still new.

PAUL. And you've rafted before huh?

DAVID. (*Continuing his fruitless labors all the while. Talking between inhales and exhales.*) Sorry? Oh, yea. What's wrong? (*A layer of annoyance sets in, what he thought would be a fun thing to do with his son is turning into something else.*)

PAUL. Just Mom said to be extra safe when I was away this week.

DAVID. (*Continuing his fruitless labors all the while. Talking between inhales and exhales.*) I'm your dad-of course this is safe. Hey, your mom and I used to do it a lot of weekends.

PAUL. Mom did this?

DAVID. (*Continuing his fruitless labors all the while. Talking between inhales and exhales.*) Sure.

The raft is not inflating.

DAVID. (*Continuing his fruitless labors all the while. Talking between inhales and exhales. Growing frustrated.*) Goddamn thing was twenty dollars.

PAUL. I don't think it's inflating.

DAVID. (*Continuing his fruitless labors all the while. Talking between inhales and exhales. Quite frustrated now.*) But it will cuz it was twenty dollars and it's brand new outta the box and I've done this before.

PAUL. Okay. (*Though he says this he clearly does not think it is true.*)

DAVID. (*Continuing his fruitless labors all the while. Talking between inhales and exhales. Bordering on angry.*) It will, trust me. I'm your dad, right? I know some stuff.

PAUL. (*Quickly trying to appease the situation, which he feels guilty for creating though it is not his fault.*) Okay.

DAVID. (*Continuing his fruitless labors all the while. Talking between inhales and exhales. Just angry now.*) Look! Your mother and I did this! Your mother did THIS! OKAY! The raft is no more inflated.

DAVID. (*Finally ceasing his fruitless labors and jumping up and away from the raft in explosion.*) Piece of shit!

PAUL. (*Stands, scared, though he has seen his father explode before, and now does not*

want to become the target.) It's okay, it's
okay. I'm not sure I was wanting to go
rafting. I'm not sure I like swimming and
stuff like that.

DAVID.   (*Ignoring his son.*) Piece of shit!
Brand new, piece of shit! Just trying to do
something… (*Trails off in his anger.*)

PAUL.   (*Reaching for his father's hand.*)
It's okay.

DAVID.   (*Jerking his hand away.*) Let go of
me!

Paul is struck dumb and simply stands with
his shoulders stooped, not knowing what to
do. David realizes his anger and what he has
just done, but does not reach out for his
son. He quells himself, though his fists
remain balled. He turns to walk up the bank
to the hill to the truck, leaving the raft
where it is, deflated. After a beat or two,
Paul follows after.

END SCENE.

<u>Sister Hall</u>

a play about
place in 3 acts

(adapted from stories
in the collection <u>Sway</u>
by Sheldon Lee Compton)

Act 1: The Heart is an Organ on Fire
Act 2: Tyrant/Superhero
Act 3: Those That Eat Shadow

Characters

<u>Sister Hall</u>: a short, dark (though may still be white) woman with white hair; her wardrobe looks something like rural farmer's wife meets gypsy mystic; probably only in her early to mid-50s, but she carries the wisdom and demeanor of the eldest among us, a result of the burden of her powers and great responsibility to those of Red Knife, Kentucky.

"The Heart is an Organ on Fire"

<u>Tracy</u>
<u>Lana</u>   > women; 3 best friends;
<u>Jules</u>   late 30s to early 40s

<u>Bruce</u>: a balding, paunchy man in his late 30s or early 40s

"Tyrant/Superhero"

<u>Roy</u>: a man, rough late 40s or early 50s; a drug addict with the appearance, clothing and ticks of a drug addict
<u>Jenny</u>: rough late 20s; sad eyes; Roy's daughter
<u>Thomas</u>: 5 or 6 or 7; Jenny's son, Roy's grandson

"Those That Eat Shadow"

<u>Tiffany</u>: a woman in her early to mid-20s; she is attractive, though bears some of the rough features of one who has sold herself

A Note on Staging and Production

The same sets can be used for Acts 1 & 2, with props changing from Tracy's table and chairs in her house, to a ratty couch and TV for Jenny's house. That said, the decoration and coloring should be distinct enough to denote two separate houses in two separate locations to the audience. Obviously the 3 separate acts can be produced and staged as 3 separate vignettes; together they paint a more complete, albeit still partial in scope, picture of our Sister Hall. Because they can be done as separate one-act plays, each act has its own title and only "Scene" is part of the label of each scene, not "Act 1, Scene1," etc.

Act 1

"The Heart is an Organ on Fire"

Scene 1

At rise we see a large single room of Tracy's
house. There is a wall toward stage right,
with a doorway to a front porch. In the
center of the room is a round table with
three chairs. While the home and furnishings
are not poor, they aren't quite lower-middle-
class either. Tracy and Bruce are eating a
dinner.

TRACY. (*Straining to make conversation with
a stupid man. She wants to date Bruce
despite his faults.*) The roof looks great.
I'm glad Lana recommended you for the job.

BRUCE. (*A little absent, not taking the
compliment.*) Yea, works done.

TRACY. Well, of course I'm not old, but
putting on shingles…well I wouldn't know
where to start. And none of the family I
have around here would step in to do
something like that.

Bruce doesn't acknowledge this at all, but
keeps eating. Tracy is frustrated and takes
a long draw of her beer.

TRACY. Now that was some work.

BRUCE. (*Continuing to eat. He talks between
bites.*) It was for sure. It's good to be
here and not be working. Just visiting.

TRACY.   (*Encouraged at his opening up.*)
Would you like another beer?

BRUCE.   Sure.

TRACY.   Right back.   (*She hops up and goes
out of the scene at stage left, returning
with a fresh beer.*)   Here we go.

BRUCE.   (*Stops eating.   He takes the beer but
he is suddenly very uncertain of what is
happening.*)   How…how long have I been here?

TRACY.   (*Taken aback.*) What?   Oh, I haven't
been paying attention.   Maybe forty-five
minutes?

BRUCE.   (*Mighty confused.*) No, but where am
I? What's my name?

TRACY.   (*Realizing Bruce has problems beyond
his obvious schleppy nature.*) What?   You're
Bruce.

BRUCE. I'm Bruce?

The light dims.   End act 1, scene 1.

Scene 2

The lights raise again and Tracy and Lana and Jules are sitting around Tracy's table drinking coffee.

LANA.   (*Almost teasing.*) The roof looks good.

TRACY.   (*Refusing enthusiasm.*) It's over my head and that'll do.

JULES.   (*Also almost teasing. Acting, as Lana, as if they know something Tracy does not.*) My, my, my what's got into you, lady?

TRACY.   (*Taking the opportunity to vent.*) I'll tell you what's wrong, this Bruce is some kind of imbecile or something. Forgets where he's at and who he is from one minute to the next. He might as well be a robot or something.

JULES. Well, we knew something wasn't exactly centered. But neither are you, Tracy! Be honest. (She winks at Lana.)

TRACY. He forgot he was here, Jules! How in the hell did he even finish my roof? I know you two said I should give him a chance, but I just can't.

LANA. Well aren't we Miss Picky? (*She winks at Jules.*) We just thought you could use him.

TRACY. Use him? And who's picky? I tried, right? I'm telling you he is mentally defective. I know you two think more of me than that.

Lana and Jules finally burst out laughing.

TRACY. What? What's the joke?

LANA. He's a corn dolly. Bruce is a corn dolly, baby girl.

TRACY. Corn dolly? I thought we were done with this kind of thing. Christ Almighty.

JULES. (*Stretches her hand from her coffee cup across the table and puts it on Jules' hand.*) Well, sweetheart, we had to do something.

The lights dim. When the lights rise a few moments later the three women are still at the table. The coffee has been cleared away and the makings for cornhusk dolls are on the table. The women busy themselves crafting in silence. The lights dim again. When the lights rise a few moments later, the women are chanting spells of incantation. The lights dim again. When the lights rise, the single corn dolly sits in the middle of the table and the three women have their coffee again.

JULES. I really and truly, truly don't see what you're so hot about. Bruce is our best one yet.

TRACY. It's just, it hasn't really worked.

LANA. That's why we're gonna call Sister
Hall, have her help.

TRACY. Oh.

Lana and Jules chuckle as Tracy remains
straight faced.

Lights down. End scene 2.

<u>Scene 3</u>

As the lights come up, Bruce is knocking on
Tracy's door. She appears from stage left
into the room, past the round table, and
opens the door. She is holding an unopened
beer bottle.

TRACY.   (*Polite but note overly polite.
Ready to be down to business.*) Come on in,
Bruce. I got you a beer.

BRUCE.   (*Still never enthusiastic, clearly
off-center in how he interacts with his
world.*) Thanks. Roof looks good.

Bruce sits in the chair at the table nearest
the door. As he sits, Tracy raises the beer
bottle over her head and smashes it down over
Bruce's head. He slumps in the chair and
falls, sprawled on his belly. The lights
dim. After several moments, the lights come
up and Bruce is now bound in the chair,
Tracy, Lana and Jules hovering over him.
Sister Hall is closing the door, having just
entered. Bruce is coming to some.

BRUCE.   (*Groggy, in pain.*) Where am I?

TRACY. (*Nicer than she was before.*) Bruce?

BRUCE.   Yes. I'm Bruce?

TRACY.   You're Bruce. So you don't know
where you are?

BRUCE.   I don't know really. I can tell you
mostly I feel like I'm waiting at a train

station for something. I don't know what the
something is, but it makes all this not
matter at all. This is a train platform, and
all I'm doing is waiting.

The three friends are confused in their
silence. Sister Hall does not make reply
either, but she does not share the confusion
or concern of the three friends.

BRUCE. (*Continuing in the absence of being
addressed again.*) That's just how things
feel. I don't think anything. You know,
like thinking about things. I guess I don't
understand all I know about it. I know I
don't like how this feels, like I said, the
train station feel. What we're talking about
right now doesn't matter. My skull all
broken means nothing. (*He's rambling in his
delirium of injury on top of his already
confused personhood.*) Everything that's real
to you is only a layover for me. And there
is no one to care, that's the worst of it,
the worst feeling. How is it I can feel
alone? How is it I even understand what
alone is, what it feels like? I know enough
to know I'm not like you, not like your
friends, the ones I first saw when I could
first see. They instructed me on what to do
and how to do it and gave me the purpose I
had up until the moment they hit me and I
left into blackness for a bit. Now I'm back
with a broken skull and with enough
understanding to feel this deep sadness. The
hardest part about being here is that I know
there's something coming that's worse.
(*Slight pause.*) None of this is fair.

TRACY. Whatever is?

Sister Hall steps forward and simply places a knuckle and thumb at the back of Bruce's neck, and Bruce sinks unconscious again.

SISTER HALL. Where's the corn dolly?

TRACY. Is it that basic, Sister? Knock him out, where's the dolly?

SISTER HALL. It's that basic.

LANA. It's here sister. (She stoops and picks the corn husk doll off the center of the table and hands it to Sister Hall.)

SISTER HALL. (*Studies the doll carefully.*) Fine work girls. A donation of the heart.

TRACY. A donation of the heart?

SISTER HALL. Yes.

TRACY. (*Suddenly skeptical though this is not her first donation or ritual.*) And also, is the plan to just push Bruce out into the river so he floats on to god knows where and end up found by some campers or whatever somewhere around German Bridge campground? (*She pauses. Sister Hall is not interested in justifying herself or answering.*) Yep, I'm figuring that's about where he'll get hung up. German Bridge.

SISTER HALL. (*Ignoring Tracy, knowing they are all in too far now. She nods to the unconscious Bruce and clutches the doll as she speaks*.) It'll take the three of you to usher the big dolly out.

With that, Sister Hall makes toward the door and exits, leaving it open, expecting her orders to be followed. She disappears stage right. Lana and Jules obediently begin to gather Bruce, each grabbing an arm and beginning to drag him toward the open door to follow. Tracy waits a minute where she is, watching her friends struggle to make this donation of the heart for her. Finally, she relents and goes along, grabbing the feet of Bruce up so he is easier to manage through the door. The three friends carry Bruce out as the lights dim.

End Scene 3.

Act 2

"Tyrant/Superhero"

Scene

At rise we see a large single room of Jenny's house. It is evening. There is wall toward stage right, with a doorway to a front porch. In the center of the room is a ratty couch and side table, a pack of cigarettes and disposable lighter on the side table. A rabbit ear box TV sits downstage centered. The home and furnishings are poor. Jenny is just settling into the sofa as Sister Hall exits the room out onto the porch, the two having said their goodbyes before the curtain rise. As Sister Hall goes down the porch steps she meets Roy just coming up the walk. He is hunched, dealing with his withdrawal but straightens up as he sees Sister Hall exiting. Sister Hall sees Roy but does not really acknowledge him otherwise, pushing on by and out of the scene. For his part, Roy is clearly fearful, or at least in awe, of Sister Hall and parts automatically to let her pass by. He gathers himself as best he can from this surprise guest, one he knows and has heard much about, leaving his daughter's house. He continues on up the porch, and knocks. Jenny, having just settled to the couch with the remote to watch TV is annoyed, and rises again to answer the door. She opens it with disappointment but minimal reaction at seeing her father.

ROY. (*Putting on his best beaming smile.*) You visitin' with Sister Hall?

JENNY.   (*Ignoring her dad's question.
Returning no expressions whatsoever.*) Why are
you here?

ROY.   (*Trying not to be put off by his
daughter's lack of welcome.*) Just visitin'
myself. Come to see how you two's getting
along.

As he talks Thomas appears at the left,
entering the room. He wears a t-shirt and
his underwear with a bath towel around his
neck, safety-pinned, like a cape. Thomas
stops when he sees his grandfather. When his
mother gives him a nodding smile, he goes
about flying around the room, running with
arms out, making swooshing sounds. He flies
back out of the room.

JENNY.   (*Buoyed by the presence of her son,
but still not emotive with her father.*) He
loves Superman. (*She sits on the couch.*)

ROY. Ahhh. Now that is a fact. Seems to be
doing pretty good. How you been?

JENNY. (*Grinning and shaking her head. It
seems like she might not respond at all, just
leave it as a rhetorical question hanging in
the air, but then she sits up straighter, and
sticks out her chin in a small gesture of
pride to reply.*) I'm off everything now. I
went to a treatment center and they weaned me
off with methadone. They were good to me,
set me up on my medical card so I was able to
pay. Still, nothing they could do about him.

(*She hooks a finger in the direction of her
departed son.*)

ROY.   Well…that's a good, good thing.
Everybody has one or two people in the family
that has that problem. not a thing to beat
yourself up about, that's for sure.

JENNY.   I don't beat myself up.

Roy thinks of sitting down, he needs to with
the withdrawal pain, but the small couch is
the only option and he reconsiders putting
himself so close to his daughter. When Jenny
sees this second guess, she inspects his eyes
for sobriety thoroughly. Whatever conclusion
she draws, she keeps to herself.

ROY. Well, good. That's a good thing.

JENNY. (*Pulls and lights a cigarette from the
pack on the side table.*) So, why are you
here?

ROY. (*Feigning injury.*) Can't a man just want
to see his daughter? His grandson?

JENNY. (*Matter of factly, not nasty. She
does not fear this man.*) No, not a man like
you. What do you want?

ROY. (*A bit taken aback at how coolly his
daughter is handling him.*) So you was
visitin' with Sister Hall? (*He kneads his
torso with a knuckle as pain blooms like a
mushroom cloud through his stomach. He
cannot wait for an answer about Sister Hall
and must get down to his business.*) Are you

getting food stamps now? (*He can no longer
look Jenny directly in the face.*)

JENNY. (*Still cool, calm, in control. She
shows no sympathies for the signs of
withdrawal.*) Oh, you want to do me a favor,
I guess. Take my stamps and trade out for
cash with some guy you know so I can pay a
couple bills? Yea. Only thing is I never
see all the money cuz you skim, maybe I don't
see any of the money because you cut out.
You've pulled this one before.

Roy's stomach pain is too much. He must sit
on the couch, but now the sit is barely
controlled, a collapse. He tries to even out
his breathing. Jenny is finally
acknowledging the situation coming to a head,
at least putting her cigarette in the ashtray
on the side table and watching her father the
whole time should he collapse into her or on
the floor. As Roy struggles down to the
couch and to manage his breathing and Jenny
sits toward him on the couch, back to stage
left, Thomas enters, dressed as before,
holding a gun. It is not a toy pistol. He
is pointing it at Roy. When he stops, Jenny
turns at the noise of her son entering,
perhaps wanting to shield him from the
spectacle of his grandfather in withdrawal
when she sees the gun and for the first time
shows emotion, letting out a small shallow
gasp. When she does so, Roy looks up from
his cramped position to see his grandson
pointing a gun at him.

ROY. Thomas! (*He grabs Jenny by the shoulders and moves her as a shield between the gun and himself.*)

Jenny easily pulls away from the drug addict's grip and throws herself toward the gun in a calm but quick motion. She grabs it raising it and her son's hands directly up, pointing at the ceiling. Thomas makes no resistance as she takes the gun from him. She takes the shells from the pistol and just lets them drop on the carpet. She puts the pistol on the side table next to the cigarettes. She picks her burning cigarette back up from the ashtray. Thomas stands staring at his grandfather, with no reaction.

ROY. (*Scarred shitless. Still grabbing his stomach in cramped pain he stands up while backing away from the couch and Thomas.*) Okay, okay, okay, okay, okay.

Roy has made his way toward the door to exit. Roy pauses at the door, feeling somewhere in himself the need to do something fatherly or grandfatherly, but his pain and the feeling he is being hunted now is too much. He bolts through the door and down the porch and out of the scene, holding his stomach in ragged breathing. Thomas goes and dutifully closes the door Roy has left swinging open. Thomas then snuggles up next to his mother on the couch. She lovingly embraces him as they settle in to watch TV.

End scene.

Act 3

"Those That Eat Shadow"

Scene

As the light rises, we are in a church, empty except for Tiffany and Sister Hall. They sit in the pews with their backs to the audience. There is a center aisle that leads to a pulpit under a giant cross. Sister Hall sits toward the back of the pews, closest the audience, while Tiffany sits toward the front in the second row. They are staggered so both are visible. They sit in silence, for a couple minutes. Tiffany goes through the machinations of personal prayer, Sister Hall watches Tiffany intently, never looking away. Tiffany finally rises and walks to the center aisle. Instead of coming back up the aisle toward the audience as if to exit, she walks to the pulpit and stares up at the cross. She begins a quiet chanting, speaking in tongues. At this, Sister Hall rises from her position and makes her way up the aisle to the pulpit under the big cross. Tiffany stops her chant and addresses Sister Hall before Sister Hall gets close to her, speaking first without turning around, still facing the cross.

TIFFANY. (*Back to the audience, looking up at the cross.*) You been watching my every move this morning, all throughout the service.

SISTER HALL. (*Never looking at the cross but only to Tiffany. As she is directly behind Tiffany she speaks.*) Tiffany Reed you seem

to be doing better. I thought one speaking
in tongues couldn't converse otherwise.

TIFFANY. (*Still not turning.*) What would
you know about it?

SISTER HALL. (*Still not looking at the
cross.*) I know all the church men around
here are talking about you and this speaking
in tongues business as the biggest thing to
hit the Holy Circuit in years. We need to
talk.

Tiffany turns to face Sister Hall. They now
face each other with the big cross and pulpit
between them.

TIFFANY. About what?

SISTER HALL. You still clean? I understand
you must still be clean being involved with
the church and all. What was your drug of
choice back in Ashland and out at the
Flatwood apartments? Pain pills mostly,
right? Some benzos. A little kitchen sink
meth with that man-child?

TIFFANY. (*Folding her arms.*) So now you
think you got the right to ask me a bunch of
questions and just show up like we've got
plans or something. I got no plans with you.
I'm going home. (*She starts to leave, then
regrets getting rude with Sister Hall.*) No
disrespect—

SISTER HALL. (*Guffaws.*) No disrespect is what
people say when they disrespecting you. You

come on with me now. (*She nods toward exiting.*)

TIFFANY. I'm not going anywhere with you. You're Sister Hall. Why in the world would I go more'n two feet anywhere with you?

SISTER HALL. Stop being a cry baby. Who got you back from Ashland and away from selling your fat ass? Who did that when your mama asked?

TIFFANY. My ass ain't fat (*She steals a second to turn her head and take a look. Satisfied she is right, she returns to addressing Sister Hall, trying to be tough but not offend someone so powerful.*) How d'you get by with this? Just demanding things of people.

SISTER HALL. How you think? Why you think? There's always more going on than people can see. Reasons for everything.

TIFFANY. Christamighty. What exactly are we talking about here Sister? You know? Okay, I owe you. Half of Port County owes you something though. It's me speaking in tongues, ain't it?

SISTER HALL. Yes, Tiffany. It's you speaking in tongues. Why you gonna come with me.

TIFFANY. (*Bouncing between a newfound power in being a church celebrity and fear of Sister Hall.*) I know it was you got me from that Emergency Room over in Ashland. But you

know, I woulda gone with anybody that woulda
got me outta that town.

SISTER HALL. I know it's an act. You're just
really good at acting. You've got a lot of
people convinced that Jesus himself plugs
into you every Wednesday and Sunday. I need
you to do something like that for me. Not
full time, mind you. But at least once a
month for the next bit. Once a week maybe.
(*Pressing on as if this is the plan, not a
pitch, not a request.*) And don't worry about
the logistics. It's fail proof. The boys
take care of all that. Also, and this should
prove most important, you get your fair
share. And I'll need you to do this tonight.

Tiffany is unsure how to answer. Sister Hall
studies her face, then puts an arm around
Tiffany turning her from the cross, huddling
the two women together in a half embrace,
staring to the back of the church toward the
audience.

SISTER HALL. When it became well known that
somewhere along Sizemore Mountain there was a
place one could visit to hear of the future,
details eventually started to spread
throughout the region. Some would say that
the oracle, a young female dressed in a
short, white dress with eyes that glowed like
fresh embers, wore a purple veil that she
would remove at some point while offering
divine messages through the vapors rising
form the earth. Some even said the oracle's
feet never touched the ground. Not due to
floating or hovering, as one would assume,
but because she was situated inside a large

type of cauldron suspended on poles above the
fissure from which the vapors emitted. (*At
this last image she gestures her free hand in
the air to indicate floating.*) Through holes
in the bottom of the cauldron vapors would
curl up the length of her body until she was
more mist than woman. (*Continues gesturing
with her free hand to paint the picture.*)
There was also a bonfire. Always a bonfire.
During the time of General Hall, my daddy,
and his tenure he had several dogs. Each
one, in turn, were brought within a few feet
of the fire and then sprinkled with ice
water. Depending on how they reacted,
General would continue the ritual or put a
stop to it then and there. The days of the
dogs have passed. I have other means now.
But back then if the dogs shivered form the
feet up, one thing happened, if they shivered
from the withers down, something else
happened. But the prophesying always started
when smoke from the bonfire joined the
vapors.

Sister Hall stops gesturing, shakes a tighter
hug on Tiffany with the arm holding her.
Tiffany is lost in this. Both bewitched by
Sister Hall and fearful of where this takes
her.

SISTER HALL. You see? You see what I'm
saying to you? Stories get told about how
the prophesying happens. Gets so no one
really knows how Sister Hall makes her magic.
(*References herself with her free hand at
this.*) They don't know if Sister Hall is a
vessel of God, or she speaks for God through
the oracle. (*Again, at the last word*

"oracle," *she makes floating vapors gestures*
with her hand.) They don't know how it
works, but that's part of it, right?

TIFFANY.   (*Intrigued, but unsure*.) Right.

SISTER HALL. So you be the oracle. You're
blessed anyway people are saying. Because
you are. Right?

TIFFANY. (*Unsure*.) Right.

SISTER HALL. So you make money. You deserve
money.

TIFFANY.   (*More certain*.) Right.

Sister Hall needs no more confirmation. She
squeezes Tiffany again a couple of times with
the arm around Tiffany. They begin to walk
away from the pulpit and cross, toward the
audience. Tiffany looks back at the cross
but Sister Hall squeezes her again,
redirecting Tiffany as they continue to walk
toward the audience. Before they reach the
end of the stage, the lights dim on Tiffany's
last line.

TIFFANY. What happened to the last oracle?

End scene.

END ALL.

95

Acknowledgments

Many, many, many thanks to Sheldon Lee
Compton for allowing his (amazing) original
work to be adapted in this form.

Reader Notes for Staging:

99

Adam Van Winkle grew up in Texoma, on both sides of the Oklahoma-Texas border. His writing has appeared in places like *Bull Fiction*, *The Dead Mule School of Southern Literature*, *Red Dirt Forum*, *Cheap Pop!*, *Crack the Spine*, *Vignette Review*, *Steel Toe Review*, *Dirty Chai*, and *Pithead Chapel*. His novel *Abraham Anyhow* was published in 2017 by Red Dirt Press, receiving a Pushcart nomination and featured in the 'If My Book' series by *Monkeybicycle*. Red Dirt Press published his novel *While They Were in the Field* in early 2019. In Fall of 2019 he released the novella *Hardway Juice* with Cowboy Jamboree Press. This is his first collection of plays, with an original play, *Two Eunices*, soon to be released. He is named for the oldest Cartwright son on *Bonanza*.